Annie and Snowball and the Shining Star

The Sixth Book of Their Adventures

Cynthia Rylant
Illustrated by Suçie Stevenson

READY-TO-READ

ALADDIN

New York   London   Toronto   Sydney

For Walker Stevenson and Jenny Freeman
—S. S.

ALADDIN
An imprint of Simon & Schuster Children's Publishing Division
1230 Avenue of the Americas, New York, NY 10020
First Aladdin hardcover edition October 2009
Text copyright © 2009 by Cynthia Rylant
Illustrations copyright © 2009 by Suçie Stevenson
ALADDIN is a trademark of Simon & Schuster, Inc.,
and related logo is a registered trademark of Simon & Schuster, Inc.
READY-TO-READ is a registered trademark of Simon & Schuster, Inc.
For information about special discounts for bulk purchases, please
contact Simon & Schuster Special Sales at 1-866-506-1949
or business@simonandschuster.com.
The Simon & Schuster Speakers Bureau can bring authors to your live event. For
more information or to book an event contact the Simon & Schuster Speakers
Bureau at 1-866-248-3049 or visit our website at www.simonspeakers.com.
Designed by Tom Daly
The text of this book was set in Goudy Old Style.
The illustrations for this book were rendered in pen-and-ink and watercolor.
Manufactured in the United States of America
2 4 6 8 10 9 7 5 3 1
Library of Congress Cataloging-in-Publication Data
Rylant, Cynthia.
Annie and Snowball and the shining star / Cynthia Rylant;
illustrated by Suçie Stevenson.
p. cm. — (Ready-to-read)
Summary: Annie's friends Henry and Mudge, and especially her rabbit, Snowball,
help her get over feeling nervous about being in a school play.
ISBN 978-1-4169-3946-7
[1. Theater—Fiction. 2. Stage fright—Fiction.]
I. Stevenson, Sucie, ill. II. Title.
PZ7.R982Ans 2009
[E]—dc22
2009011780

Contents

Christmastime

It was Christmastime
and Annie was so excited.
She called her cousin Henry
who lived next door.
"I'm going to be a star in a play!"
she said, petting her bunny, Snowball.

"You're going to be the star in a play?"
said Henry. "Wow!"

"No," said Annie, "not the star. A star.
There will be lots of stars
and I get to be one of them."
"Great!" said Henry.

"I'm a little nervous," said Annie.
"I've never been in a play before."

"Maybe you should practice," said Henry.

"Practice being a star?" asked Annie.

"Sure," said Henry.

"Mudge and I can watch."

Annie imagined Henry and Mudge
at the school play.
Mudge would want to kiss all the stars.

"Okay," said Annie.
"I'll practice at your house,
if that's okay."
"Sure," said Henry. "Come on over."

Practice!

Annie and Snowball went next door
to Henry and Mudge's house.
Henry's mom was doing laundry.
Snowball loved laundry.
She loved the warm towels.

"Is it all right if Snowball sleeps
in the towels?" asked Annie.
"Of course!" said Henry's mom.
"That's why we have white ones.
So little white bunnies can disappear!"

Annie smiled.
Snowball had disappeared,
except for her pink nose.

Annie went upstairs to Henry's room.

Henry was feeding his fish.

Mudge was helping.

When Mudge saw Annie,
he gave her a big sloppy kiss.
"Aw, Mudge," said Annie with a smile.

Henry and Mudge sat on Henry's bed
and watched Annie practice.

18

She sang a little song
and did a little dance
then took a little bow.

Henry clapped.

"Good job!" he said.

Mudge wagged.

He jumped off the bed

and kissed Annie again.

"Are you sure I did okay?"
Annie asked Henry, wiping dog drool
off her face with a hanky.
"You'll be great," said Henry.
Annie smiled.
She wasn't so nervous anymore.

Like a Star

On the night of her school play,
Annie's nerves came back.
She knew they had come back
because she had a pink blotch on her face.

Annie got pink blotches
when she was nervous.

On the way to the school,
Annie petted Snowball to calm down.
"I wish Snowball could come with me,"
Annie told her dad.

"So do I," said her dad.

"But our car is warm and she

26 has her snuggly snuggle box!"

When they arrived at the school,
Annie saw Henry and Henry's parents.
Mudge was in their car.

"I wish Mudge could come with me,"
Annie told Henry.
"So do I," said Henry.

Mudge watched Annie and Henry
go into the school.
Mudge had a shoe to chew. He was okay.

Inside, Annie went backstage
to put on her star costume.
It was sparkling silver,
and whenever she moved,
it glittered.
Annie loved it.

She loved her star costume so much that
she almost forgot about her nerves.
But when it was time to go onstage,
they came back.

Annie knew she needed
to think of something good.
So she began to think of Snowball.
She thought of Snowball being beautiful,
sparkly, and glittery, like a star.

Annie stepped onstage.

She saw her dad and Henry
and Henry's parents in the audience.

They all waved.
They looked so proud.
Suddenly Annie felt
beautiful, sparkly, and glittery.
She felt just like a star.

Annie sang her little song,
and did her little dance,
then took a little bow.

Everyone clapped
and clapped for Annie
and for all of the stars.

Annie was so happy.

After the play, Annie and Snowball
went to Henry's house for popcorn and
hot chocolate.

(Snowball and Mudge loved popcorn.)

"Were you nervous onstage?" asked Henry.

"Not really," said Annie.

"That's because you practiced," said Henry.

"Yes," said Annie.

"But Snowball helped, too."

"How?" asked Henry.
"Just by sparkling," said Annie.
And she picked up her bunny and smiled.